You do not need to read this page -
just get on with the book!

Published in 2004 in Great Britain by
Barrington Stoke Ltd, Sandeman House, Trunk's Close,
55 High Street, Edinburgh, EH1 1SR

This edition based on *CinderAlf*, published by
Barrington Stoke in 2002

ISBN 1-84299-210-4

Printed in Great Britain by Bell & Bain Ltd

## MEET THE AUTHOR – LYNNE MARKHAM

*What is your favourite animal?*
A cat
*What is your favourite boy's name?*
James
*What is your favourite girl's name?*
Helena
*What is your favourite food?*
Bacon
*What is your favourite music?*
Bach
*What is your favourite hobby?*
Gardening

## MEET THE ILLUSTRATOR – ALAN MARKS

*What is your favourite animal?*
A snow leopard
*What is your favourite boy's name?*
Thomas
*What is your favourite girl's name?*
Kate
*What is your favourite food?*
Oysters
*What is your favourite music?*
Mozart
*What is your favourite hobby?*
Cooking

# Contents

1   The Wooden Leg     1

2   CinderAlf     11

3   CinderElla     23

4   In the Woods     31

5   The Trap     39

6   In Hospital     49

7   A New Family     57

8   The End     67

# Chapter 1
# The Wooden Leg

My grandad looks just like all grandads until he goes to bed at night. Then he takes his wooden leg off and props it up at the end of the bed. The wooden foot still has a brown sock on it and a brown lace-up shoe. When I ask him what happened to his *real* leg he just shakes his head.

"Did he lose it in the war?" I ask Mum. "I can just see him being shot down by the enemy. How did he get away? Did he save a mate's life at the same time?"

"No, he was too young to be in the war," says Mum. Her face goes pink. "It was just bad luck."

"What sort of bad luck? Was his leg bitten off by a crocodile in Africa? Did he have a bad crash on a motorbike? Or did he fall out of a plane?"

"I'm not telling you," says Mum.

My younger brother Joe says the leg gives him the creeps. He says it comes alive at night when we're all in bed and marches round the house.

"*Ker-thump! Ker-thump!* Grandad's leg is on the move. The aliens sent it! There's a gun hidden inside it. If you put your hand on it when it's on the march you'll go up in flames!"

My brother Joe tells awful lies. And he's stupid. He's a thief as well. He nicks my BMX to play with his mates. He steals the flag from my space station. But worst of all, he nicks my mates.

He nicked Pete. That's when I flipped. Pete was my best mate until he met Joe. We were always together, kicking a ball or riding our bikes. We swore to be mates until the day we died. Pete was the brother I *wanted* to have. Until we bumped into Joe in the park one day.

Joe was on a skateboard. The skateboard he'd nicked from me, of course. He was doing all sorts of jumps and turns. He gave Pete a go on it and then another. Joe was having a good laugh and fooling around.

Pete was hooked. He didn't care that it was *my* skateboard. He was laughing with Joe and telling him what a great guy he was. They forgot about me until it was time to go home.

"You coming?" Pete said when it began to get dark. Then he ran off after Joe. I saw him go out of the big park gates. Then he vanished. After that Pete was out with Joe all the time.

"You can come with us if you *want* to," Joe said, grinning.

Did I need to be *invited* to go with *my* mate?

I was so angry I wanted to kill Joe. I wanted to smash my fist in his stupid face. I wanted to make sure nobody liked him again.

In the end I stormed upstairs and crashed into the first room I came to. I was crying.

"I hate Joe!" I yelled. I kicked at the door. "Everyone likes him better than me! It's not fair! He can do what he likes and people think he's cool! Well, this time I'm *really* going to get him!"

I must have been yelling for ages, and crying and hitting the wall with my fist. All at once a soft voice said, "Don't do that, Mick. You'll hurt yourself."

I spun round fast. I was in Grandad's room. He was sitting in a chair by the window. He had a look on his face I'd not seen before.

"Never say you hate your brother," he said. "Think what it would be like if you didn't have one."

"It'd be great!" I said. "I'd be Number One!  I'd get to keep all my own stuff! There'd be lots of people who liked me best! There would be no Joe to nick my mates!"

"Sit down, son," said Grandad. He patted the bed next to his chair.

I sat down with a thump and wiped my nose on my hand. I stopped crying but I was still mad. I wanted to zap Joe off the face of the earth. I never wanted to see him again.

Grandad looked hard into my face. His eyes were dark and for a moment I was scared.

When Grandad spoke again there was a sigh in his voice. He said softly, "You said you'd like it if there was no Joe. Well, suppose there was no Joe. Suppose there was no-one on your side. No-one you could count on when you'd done something bad and you were in for it. Suppose you were *really* on your own."

"Yeah!" I said. "It'd be great!"

Only it didn't feel so great to me now. Was it Grandad's sad voice that made the anger die inside me? Was it because the sun was no longer shining into the room that I began to shiver with cold?

"It might not be so great to be alone," Grandad said. "It might be hell. I know, you see. I was an only child, with no brother or sister. My parents died in a car crash when I was eight, that's three or four years younger than you are now. I was an orphan. That was just before the war started. I had no-one to call my own. Until one day everything changed. It was sort of love at first sight."

Grandad sat back in his chair and passed his hand across his face.

When he spoke again it was as if he was talking to himself and not to me.

"I want to tell you something," he said. "I want to tell you how I lost my leg."

# Chapter 2
# CinderAlf

I stared at Grandad. I felt scared, I don't know why. But I was excited, too.

"What happened?" I asked.

Grandad looked out of the window. He gave another sigh.

"Well. I told you that I was an orphan. I was sent to live with my Aunty Vera and Uncle Stan. They didn't want me. They had

two children already, you see. Two big boys called Eric and Brian.

"Uncle Stan wasn't all that bad. Most of the time he just kept out of the way. But Aunty Vera hated me. She said I cost money – money that should be spent on their two lads. She didn't even want me to wear their old clothes. She said she could have sold them and made a bit of money. She said that the money that paid for the food I ate was stolen from her boys.

"Then one day Aunty Vera found me eating some food that Eric had left on his plate. It was cold meat pie and cold gravy.

'What do you think *you're* doing, you little thief?' she yelled. She was an evil woman. 'Fetch me my pen!' she went on.

"Then Aunty Vera wrote **I AM A THIEF** in big black letters on a card and hung it

round my neck. I had to wear that card all day.

"Eric and Brian felt sorry for me. They weren't bad lads. Most of the time they played with each other. They were twins and didn't need anyone else.

'Why don't you take the card off?' they asked.

"Aunty Vera never got mad with them. They thought I was a wimp for wearing the card all day. But I was scared of Aunty. She said horrid things to me when we were on our own.

'You should be put in a home,' she'd hiss. 'You're no good to anyone. Get out of my sight.'

"I tried to keep away from her. But it was as if she could sniff me out. She always found me. She'd come up behind me and grab my collar. Her arms were like steel. Her nails dug into my neck.

'It's time to skin a rabbit,' she'd say.

"That was the thing I hated most. On Wednesdays, Aunty Vera would buy a rabbit from the butcher's shop. The rabbit would be grey and sad-looking. Its poor, dead eyes would still be open. Its paws would hang limp, the soft fur looked dull.

"My job was to help her skin it. As I tore the skin from the flesh, it sounded like a scream. I reckon it was the same scream I wanted to make. But it was coming from that dead rabbit.

'Ooh, wizard!' said Eric and Brian when they saw what we had been doing. They loved rabbit stew. They never saw the horrid bits. But I couldn't eat the stew. I'd rather go to bed hungry.

"My other job was to clean the grate and sweep out the ashes when we'd had a fire. That was all right. I'd get my arms and face all covered with ash, but I didn't care. Brian said I looked like an old man with grey hair, but Eric said, 'No he doesn't. He looks like Cinderella. Only he's a boy and his name's Alfred, so he's CinderAlf.'

"They didn't mean to be unkind. They just never thought about me. They only had time for each other. And that name stuck to me. I was CinderAlf from that day on.

"Well," Grandad went on. His voice was sad. "I was lonely, right? I'd got no-one. And that made me do what I did that day.

"It was a Tuesday morning. I got up early to clear out the grate. The ash had turned my hair pale grey. There was a pale grey light coming in from outside. Everyone else was still in bed.

"All at once this ray of sun shone into the room. I looked out at the yard. You could see a green tree poking up over the wall. There was some blue sky. The day looked too good to stay indoors. All I wanted was to get outside.

"I'd done my chores. The family were all asleep upstairs. It was safe to go out for a bit.

"I crept to the back door and drew back the bolt. It shot back with a loud bang. But no-one woke up, and in another moment I was in the back yard.

"I nipped over the wall. My heart was thumping. If Aunty found me she'd kill me and skin me like that dead rabbit.

"A song thrush was singing in a tall tree. It seemed to be telling me that something good was going to happen.

"I went down the street. I wasn't going anywhere. I was just walking because I wanted to walk and because it was sunny and spring. It was too early for a milkman to be about.

"I began to sing. Then I ran for a bit. I frisked like a horse let out in a field. I felt good. The thrush had stopped singing but I could hear something else.

"At first I thought it was someone laughing, *chuck-chuck-chuckle*. Or a clucking hen. The sound came from a shop nearby.

"I went up to the window and looked inside. There were some bright red tins on the counter with some pale green bars of soap beside them.

"The shop was still closed but the sound got louder – *chuck-chuck-CHUCKLE-CHUCK*! I went round the side to the big glass door.

In front of it there was a carrier bag made of thick brown paper. The handles were made of string.

"I went up to the carrier bag and the chuckling noise stopped. There wasn't a sound. *Something amazing is going to happen*, I thought.

"I was shaking as I leant over the bag. At first I didn't see a thing. There was just a white blob in there. Then it moved and I saw the blob had two legs and two arms. I saw a head with a pink woolly hat, and two round, blue eyes. After that the chuckling sound began again.

'Shush,' I said, softly. 'Shush. It's all right. I'm here now.'

"I was still shaking when I picked up the baby from the bag and held her for the first time in my arms."

# Chapter 3
# CinderElla

"A baby!" I said to Grandad. I was disgusted. I'd hoped for something better than that. Babies are nasty, smelly things.

Grandad went on with his story, just as if I hadn't spoken. "She was lovely. I could see that, even though her face was red and she'd a tiny fist stuck in her mouth. When I picked her up she stopped chuckling. She looked at me out of her big blue eyes. That's

when I knew she was meant for me. There was even a note pinned to her jumper. It said: *Please take care of my little girl. I can't.*

"When I read the note I got a lump in my chest, a kind of deep sadness. Nobody wanted the baby. She hadn't a friend in the world. She was on her own – like me.

"The lump in my chest got bigger and bigger. Then all at once I got this great idea. I would keep the baby. I knew she wasn't my real sister. But she was better than that. Better than Aunty Vera and Uncle Stan and the twins. She just made the world seem grand.

"I put her back in the carrier bag. There was a baby's bottle in there, too. I picked up the bag and set off down the street.

"At first, I didn't know where I was going. I just walked and walked. I could feel the baby bumping about in the bag, but she didn't start to cry. She seemed to know what I was doing and that I was going to take care of her.

"By then the street had woken up. The milkman was clinking bottles about. I could hear the sound of the trams. It made me scared I might be seen. That Aunty Vera might appear in her nightie and drag me back to her house. Then I'd never see the baby again.

"I walked faster and faster. I still didn't know where I was going. Then I saw a lot of small gardens in a field. You could see rows of leeks and carrots and there were sheds made out of scraps of wood and old front doors.

"I slowed down. Some of the gardens were no longer cared for. One of these had a shed in it.

"I walked up to it and went inside. There was an empty crate on the floor. It said BEST BANANAS on the side. I put the baby into it. It was just the right size for her. She kicked her legs and smiled.

"I started to grin. I had always wanted the world to be great and now it was. There was someone who needed me.

"When she fell asleep, I tip-toed out of the shed and went home. I jumped up and down on the way. When I got home Aunty Vera was there.

'What have *you* been doing?' she asked. She hated me to be happy.

"I ate a slice of bread and dripping and put the other slice in my pocket. Then I washed the dishes and set off for school.

"Only I never got there. You see, I went back to the shed. And the baby was still fast asleep in her crate. I kept looking at her. I was amazed that she could really be mine.

"What she needed now was a proper name. I thought of Susan and Sarah and Jane. None of them sounded right. She was poor and unwanted like me.

"I called her Ella. We'd be Cinder*Alf* and Cinder*Ella*. It was like being a real brother and sister. We'd belong to each other.

"I stroked her face very gently with my finger. Then I said her name out loud for the first time. 'Ella.' I was a bit scared. I didn't know very much about babies.

"How would I look after her? How would I get her food and clothes? How would I make sure no-one found her?

"And what would happen if Aunty Vera got to know about her?"

# Chapter 4
# In the Woods

"Did Aunty Vera find out?" I asked.

"She might have done," Grandad said. "But before she could we ran off to the woods. It was before they built that new estate. There were woods all around us in those days."

"Great!" I said.

In my mind the woods were dark and deep. You could have a gang there. You could make a fire out of twigs and leaves. You could have fun.

"It wasn't like that," Grandad went on, as if he knew what I was thinking. "It wasn't fun at all. It was hard. We were hungry all the time.

"I made a small shelter for us out of branches and leaves. After that, I made Ella a cradle, just a hollow in the soft earth, lined with moss. She looked lovely in it.

"But I was scared to leave her there in case someone found her. Sometimes people came to the woods to walk their dogs. But what could I do? There was nowhere else to go.

"I left her every day while I went out and stole. I stole a blanket and some nappies off a line. I stole bread from the baker's van. I stole milk from doorsteps and fruit from gardens. I stole eggs from a hen-house in a farmer's field.

"No-one seemed to be looking for me. Aunty Vera must have been glad to be rid of me. We were alone in the woods.

"It rained a lot. I had to steal an umbrella for us. I almost got found out that time.

"I saw some umbrellas near an open door and I crept up and grabbed one. Then I heard this yell.

'You, boy! What are you doing there? Parker! Come quick – we have a thief!'

"It was a lady who was yelling like that. But it was a big man in a dark suit who came out of a back room.

'You little devil!' he yelled at me in a posh voice. 'I'll beat you black and blue when I catch you!'

"He tried to grab me, but I was faster than him. I shot out of the door, but I kept the umbrella. After that I ran like the wind, up and down the back streets of the town.

"When at last I stopped I was somewhere I didn't know. My heart was thumping. People in the street were looking at me.

"Then I saw a policeman walking down the street towards me. I thought he was coming to get me. So I ran off again and this time I ended up back in the woods.

"For the rest of the day I was too scared to go out. We sat under the umbrella, me and Ella, under the dripping trees.

"That night we were both too hungry to sleep. She was crying all the time.

"This is what happened next. I'd gone out to look for food again, but people had taken their milk off their doorsteps. It was getting warmer, and they didn't want their milk to sit out in the sun. So I had to go a long way to find some. I walked and walked.

"In the end I came to some shops. One of them was a Post Office. There was a big red letterbox outside. There was a poster pinned up on the wall above it.

"I had a look at the poster as I went past. I stood still with shock. Then I felt as if I had been punched in the chest.

"The poster said:

WANTED – HAVE YOU SEEN THIS BOY?

And it had a photo of me."

# Chapter 5
# The Trap

"Wow!" I said. My grandad was a wanted man! It was almost as good as getting eaten by a crocodile!

Grandad said, "It was an old photo. The boy looked younger than me, and cleaner. But you could tell it was me. It even had my name written there: Alfred Packard.

"The photo made me feel sick inside. I felt that everyone was looking at me. Even the old ladies going for stamps. I felt like a thief.

"So I ran away. I always seemed to be running away. Except when I was with Ella. Then everything slowed down and life was more gentle. As if we were living in another world.

"After I'd seen the photo, I ran back to Ella. I was panting and my chest hurt. When I got back, Ella looked smaller and thinner than ever. Her blanket was damp. She had nasty, red patches on her skin.

"Ella began to cry a lot. Not a loud cry, more a gentle bleat. Like an animal in pain. The crying broke my heart. When I picked her up she stopped crying, but her breathing was all wheezy.

"It sounded like mine. It was as if her chest was all blocked up. She wheezed and her nose ran. Her hands felt cold.

"*We are meant for each other*, I thought. *I can't give her up. It would be like cutting off an arm or a leg.*

"So I went on stealing food and trying to get her to eat. But she wouldn't. She just cried and wheezed.

'Come *on*, Ella,' I used to say. 'Please eat this. Just for me.'

"I even stole a toy for her. It was a blue velvet dog with long white ears. The dog lay on her chest like a dead thing.

'What can I *do?*' I asked her, scared.

"I was in a panic by now. I tried to cuddle her and keep her warm. I knew I had to give her up. But still I might not have done it then. I might not even have done it at all.

"But something else happened. Something so terrible I can hardly tell you."

Grandad was silent and his face went blank. He was seeing something I couldn't see.

"What happened?" I said softly. I was almost too scared to ask.

Grandad spoke again. His voice was hard and low. "I was out one day and I was stealing eggs.

"I went to a place I'd not been to before. It was a small farm set behind some trees. You could see the hens scratching around. The hen-houses were rotten and falling down.

"I went over the fence and into the trees. The grass under them was very tall and I was small and skinny. I was moving with care. I didn't want to be seen. I had nearly got to the hens.

"All at once I heard this *crack*! Just like a gun going off. Then there was this pain in my leg. It was so bad I almost fainted. I looked down and saw I was in a trap.

"The teeth of the trap were digging into my leg. Blood was running down it in a thick, bright stream. The pain was – well ..."

Grandad stopped again. He passed a hand across his face.

"... it was like nothing I've felt before or since. I think the teeth had almost got to the bone.

"I tried to pull the teeth of the trap apart. But they seemed to be locked in place. I pulled and pulled, but they wouldn't budge. Then I started yelling, 'Help me! Help!'

"No-one came. My voice was thin and weak.

"*I'm going to die*, I thought. But then something magic happened.

"I was pulling in a feeble way at the metal trap when it gave a click. The teeth came apart an inch or two. It wasn't much. But it was enough for me to pull myself free.

"After that I began to struggle back to the woods. My leg was still bleeding and turning blue. I was fighting my way through the grass, crying and panting as I went.

"Still, I made it back to Ella.

"She was silent when I got there. Not even bleating.

'Ella?' I said. 'Don't fret. I'm here.'

"I took my shirt off and tied it round my leg. But it hurt so much that I could hardly breathe. And it had begun to rain again. Without my shirt I was freezing cold.

"I knew it was the end for us. My leg was swelling. It hurt me to breathe. And *my* skin had funny red patches all over, just like Ella's. I couldn't go out any more to steal for us.

"I picked Ella up. 'I'm so sorry,' I said.

"I put her back down. I couldn't look at her face. The pain at leaving her again was worse than the pain in my leg.

"It still hurts me when I think about it.

"I crept away. Somehow I got to some shops. When I crept in at the door everyone stared.

"The shopkeeper looked up with his hands on the till. A lady moved away from me.

'I'm the boy on the poster,' I said.

"The lady gave a scream.

"Then all hell broke loose."

# Chapter 6

# In Hospital

Grandad stopped again. He seemed about to drown in a black pool of sadness. "Well," he said at last. "They called the police and an ambulance. The police car came with its bell ringing.

"The shopkeeper made a fuss of me. 'You've been in the newspapers for the last two weeks. Everyone thought you were dead,' he said.

"The ambulance came. They put a blanket round me. But I wouldn't let them take me away.

'You've got to go and find Ella!' I said.

"They thought the pain had done odd things to me. That I was not quite right in my mind and didn't know what I was saying.

'Shush,' they said. 'You'll be all right.'

"They picked me up but I kicked and bit. 'Find Ella!' I said. 'She's in the woods. Let me go and I'll take you there.'

"Of course they didn't know about Ella. They thought I was just making her up.

"But I kicked and yelled until I was blue in the face. In the end they thought it was best to go along with me. They put me in a black police car. An ambulance followed after us.

'Right. Take us to this kid,' they said. And they smiled to each other over my head.

"We drove and drove down all the wrong roads. I was muddled and angry. I was in pain. I couldn't find the right way. It all looked different from a police car.

"When we got to the woods I limped out. A policeman had to hold me up. We pushed our way through the trees until we came to where Ella was.

"I heard her bleating, but I still didn't look.

'Poor little thing!' a policeman gasped.

"The words were like a knife in my heart.

"I was too sad even to cry for her.

"They put a blanket round her and took her to the ambulance. I didn't go with her, I just stood there, shocked and stunned.

'Come on, lad,' they said. 'Your turn now.' But I didn't move until Ella had gone.

"I knew, you see, that this was the end. That she'd go to the hospital and that she'd be taken away from me. That I wasn't going to see her, ever again.

"Later, I let them take me away. I went to the same hospital, to a big children's ward. I lay in bed with my leg throbbing, but they said they'd got to cure my chest first.

'How's Ella?' I kept asking, over and over again.

'She's doing all right. You just try to get well again yourself.'

"When my chest was better, they said my leg had to go.

"It was so badly infected that they had to cut it off. I didn't care. Not without Ella.

"Aunty Vera came to see me with Eric and Brian. Aunty stared at me with her evil little eyes.

'Don't think I'll have you back to live with us!' she said. 'You'll come to a bad end. I'm not going to look after you any more.'

"Brian and Eric didn't look at me or at their mum.

'Sorry, mate,' Eric said when they left. I never saw either of them again.

"I didn't *want* to go back and live with them, but what was going to happen to me?

"I didn't care. I was weak and unhappy. I kept seeing Ella in my dreams. I could hear her cry.

"One day they told me she'd been adopted.

'She's got a nice new mum and dad,' they told me. 'Don't fret. She'll have a good life.'

"I knew it was the best thing for her, but I was still very unhappy. And I wanted proof that Ella was really OK. Then one day a young nurse came over to me.

"She looked around to see if anyone could see us and then she put a photo into my hand. 'Don't tell anyone I gave you this,' she hissed.

"The photo was of Ella. She looked plump and clean. She was looking at me and she seemed to be trying to tell me something.

"I put the photo under my pillow. And that night I slept for the first time in weeks.

"When I woke up I was feeling better. The sun was shining. I was taken to be fitted for a wooden leg. After that my luck got better. But where would I go when I left hospital?

"Then something happened. Something good. And I was never to be so unhappy again."

# Chapter 7
# A New Family

Grandad stopped talking. He was smiling. The smile made him look different.

I tapped his arm. "What happened?" I asked.

"Well, there was this lady and her husband who'd read about me. They'd seen my photo in the newspaper. They wanted to

find out more about me. They had no children of their own.

"One day a thin lady came to see me. She wore a brown felt hat. She stared at me as I lay in bed. Then she said, 'There's some very good people who might like to have you. You must be nice to them when they come and see you. You can't go and live with your aunty again. She doesn't want you. She thinks you're a bad lad.'

"The thin lady talked to me very slowly and in a loud voice, as if I was stupid.

'You're to smile at them,' she went on. 'Be polite. If you're good they might want to take you home.'

"I was scared and fed up by what she said. Who was she, anyway? *I* didn't know. And would the new people be as bad as my aunt and uncle? Would they just want

someone to do all the jobs around the house?

"I made a face at the thin lady and she marched out of the ward. You could hear her stomping away down the corridor. A door slammed.

"Two days later the thin lady was back again.

'Mr and Mrs Ross are here. Remember what I said to you. Be polite. Smile at them.'

"She spoke to me just like my aunt used to do, as if my feelings didn't matter. So when Mr and Mrs Ross came in, I glared at them. I didn't say a word.

'You must be Alfred,' the lady said. She had a nut-brown face and rosy cheeks. 'Poor Alfred. You've had a horrid time. Well,

never mind. You'll be all right now. Say
hello to my husband. He's a bit shy.'

"Mr Ross's neck was too long. He wore
glasses. His hands shook.

'How do, son,' he said. His face was very
red. He gave a gulp and came up to my bed.
He held out his hand to me.

'Well, go on then, Alfred,' Mrs Ross said.
'Shake his hand or he'll be upset.'

"Slowly I put out my hand. Mr Ross's
hand took mine. It felt warm and dry.

'There now!' Mrs Ross said. 'That didn't
hurt much, did it, lads?'

"She pulled a chair up and sat down
beside me. Then *she* took my hand and held
it tight. She spoke to me in a very soft and
kind voice.

'I know we're not Ella. But we can still be your friends, Alfred. Is that all right?'

"I nodded. Somehow I didn't feel angry any more. Mrs Ross still held my hand.

"In the end, I went home with them. Only not at once. It took a week or two to sort things out.

"I had to learn to use my new leg first. I had to learn to walk again."

"And did you ever see Ella again?" I asked.

Grandad shook his head. "Only in my mind. But she's never really gone away. She's inside my head like a patch of sun."

"Yeah." I looked at the floor. I didn't know whether to feel happy or sad. "Can I see Ella's photo now?" I asked.

Grandad fumbled around in the drawer by his bed and took out an old wallet. Inside the wallet was the photo in a leather frame.

Ella was just like any other baby, but the eyes were a bit wider. And there was something different about the chin.

"She looks like our mum!" I said, amazed.

"Your mum looked just like her when she was born. It was magic. We called your mum Joy, because that's what she was to us."

Grandad held the photo in his hand and gazed at it. He seemed to have forgotten I was there.

Very slowly I got to my feet. *Grandad wants to be alone*, I thought. But when I got to the door he looked up and spoke.

"Take care of your brother! D'you hear me?"

I nodded and went back downstairs.

# Chapter 8
# The End

A few days later, Pete came round. "Is Joe in?" he asked me.

I gave a shrug. "Dunno."

"We were going to go off round the park – can he have your bike? His bike's too small for him."

I was going to say something and then I didn't. What had Grandad said? *Take care of your brother.* It made me think.

Joe's OK. Most of the time. We mess about. We tease our mum. When mum's cross he's on my side.

If Joe went away I'd be really upset. I'd miss him like an arm or a leg. He's like no-one else. He can't help being so popular.

"Well?" said Pete. "Can Joe have your bike, just for this morning?"

I glared at him and folded my arms. "No!" I yelled. "He flaming well can't! He'll have to use his own stupid bike!"

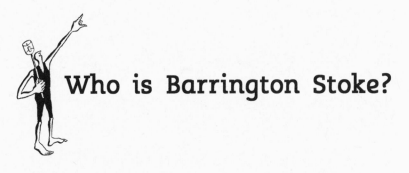

# Who is Barrington Stoke?

Barrington Stoke went from place to place with his lamp in his hand. Everywhere he went, he told stories to children. Some were happy, some were sad, some were funny and some were scary.

The children always wanted more. When it got dark, they had to go home to bed. They went to look for Barrington Stoke the next day, but he had gone.

The children never forgot the stories. They told them to each other and to their children and their grandchildren. You see, good stories are magic and they can live for ever.

## If you loved this story, why don't you read ...

# Resistance

## by Ann Jungman

Do you ever disagree with your parents? Jan is ashamed when his Dutch father sides with the Germans during the Second World War. Only Elli is his friend. Can Jan find a way to help the Resistance?

# 4u2read.ok!

## If you loved this story, why don't you read ...

# Bungee Hero

## by Julie Bertagna

Are you afraid of high places? Adam is terrified of them. So why then would he do a bungee jump to earn money for charity? It is only after old Mr Haddock tells him his sad story that Adam decides to have a go. But will he just be too scared to do it?

# 4u2read.ok!

You can order this book directly from our website
www.barringtonstoke.co.uk

## If you loved this story, why don't you read ...

# Hostage

## by Malorie Blackman

Can you imagine how frightened you would be if you were kidnapped? Angela is held to ransom and needs all her skill and bravery to survive.

# 4u2read.ok!

# If you loved this story, why don't you read ...

# The House with No Name

## by Pippa Goodhart

Can secrets live on after death? Jamie moves into a house that has been empty for thirty-five years. He discovers a tragic secret from the past. Find out what Jamie comes across in the House with No Name.

# 4u2read.ok!

# If you loved this story, why don't you read ...

# Tod and the Sand Pirates

## by Anthony Masters

Have you ever had to fight for your life? The whole world is suffering from a lack of water. There is a huge fuel shortage too. Tod and Billy are looking for a new water supply, when pirates take them prisoner. How will they escape?

# 4u2read.ok!

You can order this book directly from our website
www.barringtonstoke.co.uk